Ursula tried to swim faster, but the boats were all around her and she began to feel very scared. All at once a hand gripped her firmly by the scruff of the neck, hauled her out of the water, and dumped her in a dripping heap in the bottom of a boat.

'Bloomin' heck. It's a bear,' said a voice in astonishment.

For Ursula is an ordinary little girl with one very special secret – she can turn herself into a real live bear. In this hilarious new adventure, Ursula soon discovers that rivers and boats mean trouble for bears . . .

Ursula Sailing

Ursula Sailing

Sheila Lavelle
Illustrated by Thelma Lambert

YOUNG CORGI BOOKS

URSULA SAILING

A YOUNG CORGI BOOK 0 552 524484

Originally published in Great Britain in 1984 by
Hamish Hamilton Children's Books

PRINTING HISTORY
Young Corgi edition published 1987

This book is set in 14/18 pt Garamond
by Colset Private Limited, Singapore.

Young Corgi Books are published by Transworld Publishers
Ltd., 61–63 Uxbridge Road, Ealing, London W5 5SA, in
Australia by Transworld Publishers (Australia) Pty. Ltd., 15–23
Helles Avenue, Moorebank, NSW 2170, and in New Zealand
by Transworld Publishers (N.Z.) Ltd., Cnr. Moselle and
Waipareira Avenues, Henderson, Auckland.

Made and printed in Great Britain by
The Guernsey Press Co. Ltd., Guernsey, Channel Islands.

Ursula Sailing

Chapter One

Ursula didn't look different from other girls. She had ordinary brown hair, a nice, ordinary face and a few freckles on her ordinary nose. She wore plain, ordinary knitted jumpers and jeans and skirts and vest and knickers and woolly hats and socks and wellies in the winter just like any other ordinary girl.

But Ursula had a secret.

One day, in a book in the library, Ursula had found a magic spell. A currant bun, a spoonful of porridge oats and another of honey. Put them all together with a few magic words and the most astonishing thing would happen. Ursula could turn herself into a real, live bear.

Ursula didn't dare tell this secret to anybody except two very special friends, Mrs Martinez and Mr Blomeyer. It wasn't the sort of thing people would understand. Especially kind, comfortable Aunt Prudence, with whom Ursula lived. She would have been horrified if anyone had told her about Ursula's adventures as a bear. Aunt Prudence believed that Ursula was just a nice, ordinary little girl. And

Ursula thought it was better to let her think so.

Early one sunny morning Ursula heard the postman's knock. She was in such a hurry to reach the door that she almost fell down the stairs.

'Goodness, child. What a lot you've got,' said Aunt Prudence, peering over the bannister in her dressing gown. Ursula, her arms full of letters and packages, beamed up at her from the hall.

'Twelve cards, three parcels, and a great big box thing from Canada,' she said. 'Everybody has remembered my birthday.'

'You reminded them often enough,' said Aunt Prudence, coming downstairs and kissing Ursula's cheek. 'There's one more from me in the kitchen.'

Aunt Prudence put the kettle on while Ursula opened her post. She stood the twelve cards in a row on the mantelpiece and began to open the parcels. Off came the wrappers and out came a new yellow cardigan from Aunt Prudence, a water-colour paintbox and brushes, a boring old sewing kit for making yourself a nice sensible apron, which Ursula made a rude face at, and a big, fat book called The Adventures of Bartholomew Bear. This pleased

Ursula much more, because she loved bears better than anything else in the world.

Ursula had left the biggest parcel until last. She looked at the large, flat box with the Canadian stamps on it and tried to guess what it could be.

'Go on then. Open it,' said Aunt Prudence. 'It's from Uncle Angus and Aunt Grace, I think.'

Without wasting any more time Ursula pulled off the wrappings and lifted the lid.

'Oh,' she breathed. 'Look, Aunt Prudence. It's an aeroplane.'

Aunt Prudence began to lay the table for breakfast.

'It's not an aeroplane. It's a glider,' she said. 'It hasn't got an engine. Funny sort of present, anyway.'

Ursula didn't think so. She gently lifted the glider from its box and stroked the long silver wings.

'It's beautiful,' she said, her eyes shining. 'I'll fly it on the common straight after breakfast. Can I take a picnic lunch and stay out all day?'

'Well, mind it doesn't end up in the river,' said Aunt Prudence, pouring Ursula's cornflakes into a bowl.

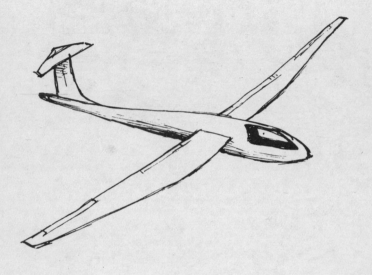

Chapter Two

It was a perfect day for flying a glider. The sun was shining, the sky was blue and there was a strong, steady wind. Ursula chose a good spot, well away from the trees and the river, where there was a steep hill to give her more height. She climbed to the top of the hill and dumped her picnic bag down on the grass. Then she stood on tiptoe and launched the glider as high as she could into the air.

Ursula held her breath and watched. The breeze lifted the glider into the sky, making it rise and soar like a bird. The silver wings shone in the sun and it wasn't long before a crowd of people had gathered to watch.

'It's great,' said two small boys, their faces green with envy. 'Bet it's not really yours.' Ursula couldn't help feeling proud.

The glider finally floated to the ground some distance away and Ursula ran to pick it up. Then she climbed back up the hill and launched it all over again. It was the best birthday present Ursula had ever had.

She was having such a busy time watching the glider and running down the hill to collect it that she didn't see the great, dark cloud creeping along the edge of the sky. It was only when the sun vanished suddenly behind it and people had begun to leave in

a hurry that Ursula noticed the change in the weather.

'There's a storm coming,' warned a young man in a leather jacket, jogging by with an Alsatian on a lead. 'I'd clear off home if I were you.'

Ursula stared up at the black sky. A sudden great gust of wind nearly blew her over and she felt big spots of rain on her face.

'I'd better run, I suppose,' she sighed.

And then Ursula did a very silly thing.

'I'll just have one more go first,' she said to herself. And she ran up the hill once more.

As soon as Ursula reached the top she realized her mistake. But by then it was too late. The blustery wind was too strong for her. It tore the glider from her grasp and flung it like a feather towards the clouds.

The rain trickled down Ursula's face, but she hardly noticed. Her eyes were fixed on the silver shape in the sky as it was tossed about by the wind, plunging first

one way and then the other, sometimes
plummeting like a stone and then suddenly soaring higher than ever.

'It'll never come down,' wailed Ursula in despair.

But at last the wind steadied for a moment and the glider began to descend, coming down fast in a straight line towards the trees near the river. Ursula grabbed her picnic bag and set off after it at a run.

'Don't go in the river,' she gasped, out of breath. 'Please don't land in the river.'

The glider didn't land in the river. It jammed itself in a dead branch at the very top of the tallest sycamore tree on the river bank. And there it stuck, a hundred feet from the ground.

Chapter Three

Ursula flung herself down under the tree
and a few tears mingled with the rain on
her face. Nobody could climb a tree as big
as this one, she was sure. It must be the
biggest tree in the world. Even its lowest
branches were too high for her to reach.
And shaking it wouldn't do any good,

either. You might as well try to shake an
elephant.

Ursula leaned her back against the trunk
and sighed.

'I'll just have to stay here until the tree falls down,' she told herself stubbornly. 'It might take fifty years or so. But I'm not going home without my glider.'

After a while the rain stopped, the wild wind quieted a little and a gleam of sunshine lit up the wet leaves. A few white sails appeared from the nearby sailing club and began to race up and down the river.

'I might as well eat my lunch, anyway,' said Ursula, drying her face on her hanky and feeling better at the thought of pork pie and smoky bacon crisps.

Ursula was unpacking the picnic bag when all at once her eyes grew wide. As a special birthday surprise Aunt Prudence had made Ursula's favourite treat. A large currant bun, filled with a mixture of porridge oats and honey.

Ursula stared at the bun. Then she did a little jig of excitement.

'Bears can climb,' she breathed. 'Bears can climb better than anybody. Almost as good as monkeys, bears are.' And she quickly took a bite.

A currant bun had never tasted so good. And Ursula was careful not to forget the magic words.

'I'm a bear, I'm a bear, I'm a bear,' she mumbled as she chewed. 'I'm a bear, I'm a bear, I'm a bear.'

Ursula finished the last crumb, hid the rest of her picnic under a gorse bush, and then lay down under the tree to wait for the spell to work. And if the young man with the dog had walked by a few moments later he would have seen a most astonishing sight. A small brown bear, dancing gleefully about in the grass.

Ursula had turned once again into
Ursula Bear.

Chapter Four

Climbing that great tree was easy for a
bear, Ursula thought, as her strong little
claws found all the best cracks in the bark.
She pulled herself steadily upwards,
pausing now and then to get her breath
back and to brush a few wet leaves from
her fur. Once she met a surprised-looking

squirrel, who chattered in alarm and threw a twig at her, and in a fork of a branch she found a nest of baby robins waiting for their dinner.

At last she reached the very top of the tree. She took a peep down at the shining river far below, where the sailing boats bobbed like toys in the bath. Then, as she crawled out from among the leaves onto a bare, dead bough, Ursula saw the glider, still stuck fast among the twigs.

The old branch began to creak warningly as Ursula inched forward on her stomach towards the glider. She paused, clinging tightly in alarm. The glider was still out of reach, so after a moment Ursula edged along a tiny bit further. The branch cracked and groaned even more, and Ursula almost stopped breathing. But now

she could just reach the glider's tail. She
stretched out her paw as far as she could
and with a desperate tug she managed to
dislodge it from the twigs.

Ursula turned and quickly sent the glider skimming back over the common. She just had time to see it land safely in a tall patch of bracken before, with a loud, splintering snap, the branch broke. Ursula came tumbling down out of the tree and landed with a huge splash in the river.

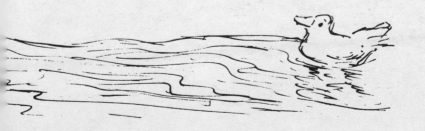

Chapter Five

Ursula coughed and spluttered as the water closed over her head. But bears are good swimmers, and it wasn't long before she got her breath back and began to swim steadily towards the bank.

'Lucky I fell in the water,' she told herself thankfully. 'And not in one of those prickly gorse bushes.'

Ursula's troubles were still not over, however. She had fallen right into the middle of the boat race, and she almost jumped out of her furry skin as a large shape suddenly loomed through the water towards her. And then she found them coming at her from all directions, whizzing past her ears and just managing to miss one another as they swerved to avoid her bobbing brown head.

The sailors craned their necks to see what was getting in their way.

'It's a dog,' shouted one on the yachtsmen. 'It must have fallen in the river.'

'It's going to cause an accident in a minute,' yelled another. 'Why doesn't somebody do something?'

Ursula tried to swim faster, but the

boats were all around her and she began to
feel very scared. All at once a hand gripped
her firmly by the scruff of the neck, hauled
her out of the water, and dumped her in a
dripping heap in the bottom of a boat.

'Bloomin' heck. It's a bear,' said a voice in astonishment, and Ursula saw that her rescuer was a boy of about twelve, in a blue sailing jacket. 'Look, dad,' he said. 'It's a little cub. How did he get in the water?'

The man at the tiller peered at Ursula.

'Good lord, so it is,' he said, scratching his head in surprise.

'Somebody's pet, I suppose. Must have fallen off a cruiser.' He pushed the tiller and began to turn the boat upstream. 'We'd better take him up to the Thames River Police at Cookbridge.'

The sails filled with wind and the boat began to tack back and forth up the river, leaving the others to finish their race in peace. Ursula cowered in the bottom of the boat, feeling cold and wet and miserable. And the thought of being locked up

in a police station didn't cheer her up at
all.

But the sun and the breeze quickly
dried Ursula's fur, and it wasn't long
before she found that she was beginning to
enjoy herself. It was nice to see the sun

sparkling on the water, to feel the wind on her face, and to watch the boy and his father as they steered and tacked and pulled bits of rope.

They sailed further and further upstream, and although Ursula was enjoying the sailing she began to feel more and more worried. The further they took her away from home, the harder it would be to get back. And what would happen if the River Police did lock her up? What would Aunt Prudence say when she didn't turn up at teatime?

'Cookbridge Lock ahead,' said the boy suddenly. And Ursula saw that they were approaching a narrow channel in the river, with a big wooden gate, a bridge and a lock-keeper's cottage. She sat up quickly and her bright black eyes shone. This

could be her chance to escape.

The lock-keeper almost fell in the water when he saw Ursula sitting in the boat, but he opened the lock gates for them and they sailed in.

'Get the mainsail down,' said the boy's father, and the boy unfastened a string on the mast. The big sail slid down into the bottom of the boat, burying Ursula in its folds.

Steering a sailing boat through a lock is a slow, tricky business. The boy and his father were kept very busy for the next few minutes, and Ursula peeped out from under the sail, watching for just the right moment.

At last it came. As soon as the lock was filled with water and everybody's eyes were fixed on the opening gates, Ursula scrambled out and leapt ashore. And nobody noticed a small brown figure scurrying rapidly away through the undergrowth along the river bank.

The afternoon was almost over when a

weary little bear finally arrived back at the
sycamore tree. But all was well, and the
picnic bag was still where Ursula had left it
hidden in a bush. The glider took longer
to find, as all the patches of bracken
looked the same, but at last she spotted a
silver wingtip sticking out from the ferns.
Ursula pounced on the glider with a cry of
delight and scampered off home as fast as
her short, furry legs would carry her.

Chapter Six

Mrs Martinez and Mr Blomeyer were Ursula's two best friends. They were sitting in Aunt Prudence's cottage later that afternoon, sipping tea from blue china cups and waiting for Ursula to come home.

'I can't think what can have happened to the child,' fussed Aunt Prudence. 'She

promised to be home for tea.'

Mr Blomeyer wasn't listening. His eyes were fixed on the lowest pane of the french window and his mouth was hanging open in astonishment. He had just glimpsed an anxious little face peering through the glass. A brown furry face, with round ears and a black shiny nose.

Mr Blomeyer swallowed the rest of his tea so fast he almost choked. He leapt out of his chair and made the best china rattle alarmingly.

'Er . . . must go . . .' he stammered. 'Sorry . . . back in a minute.' And he rushed out, leaving Aunt Prudence and Mrs Martinez gazing at one another in surprise.

Ursula was stowing the glider and the picnic bag safely away in the garden shed when Mr Blomeyer grabbed her by the paw. She was very lucky that he, and not Aunt Prudence, had seen her first. Mr Blomeyer wasted no time in telling her so.

'This really is a bit much,' he said

crossly, hurrying Ursula down the street and round the corner to his own house. 'I don't like this dangerous game of yours. And now I suppose I'm going to have to cook beefburger and chips to turn you back into yourself again.'

Mr Blomeyer's untidy kitchen was soon filled with the delicious smell of frying. When the food was ready Ursula quickly gobbled it down, standing at the kitchen table and growling the magic words as she ate.

'Raeb a m'I, Raeb a m'I, Raeb a m'I,' she mumbled, wiping tomato ketchup from her furry chin. 'Raeb a m'I, Raeb a m'I, Raeb a m'I.'

And in no time at all she was herself
again, much to Mr Blomeyer's relief and
delight. Ursula told him everything that
had happened to her as they hurried back
to Aunt Prudence's house together.

'So here you are at last, young lady,'

tutted Aunt Prudence when they went in. 'What have you been up to all day, may I ask?'

Ursula grinned at Mr Blomeyer and Mrs Martinez. She took a deep breath.

'My glider got stuck up a tree so I magicked myself into a bear and climbed up the tree but then I fell in the river and got rescued by a sailing boat and I jumped ashore and ran home and then I magicked myself back again and here I am.'

Aunt Prudence stared at Ursula. Then she began to laugh. 'Go and wash your hands for tea,' she said. 'And we'll have no more of your nonsense.' She patted Ursula's cheek fondly as she went out.

'What an imagination that child's got,' said Aunt Prudence, smiling and pouring herself another cup of tea.

URSULA CAMPING

BY SHEILA LAVELLE
ILLUSTRATED BY THELMA LAMBERT

Ursula is an ordinary girl – with one special difference. If she eats a currant bun, stuffed with a mixture of porridge oats and honey, and recites a magic spell, she can turn herself into a real, live, little bear!

When she runs up against trouble from her two cousins, Ian and Jamie, while on a camping holiday in the New Forest, Ursula finds that being able to change herself into a bear can be very useful indeed . . .

0 552 524476

YOUNG CORGI

MIDNIGHT PIRATE

BY DIANA HENDRY
ILLUSTRATED BY JANET DUCHESNE

'Oh Pirate, dear little Pirate,' whispered Ida,
'you can't stay here. The Aunts don't want a
kitten.'

Nothing Ida could say would make the Aunts
change their minds and it seemed as though the
tiny kitten she had found under the holly bush
would have to stay out in the cold and wet,
unloved by anyone.

But the kitten had other ideas and even the
Aunts became involved in what happened
next . . .

0 552 524174

YOUNG
CORGI

DRAGON FIRE

BY ANN RUFFELL
ILLUSTRATED BY ANDREW BROWN

Gribble, the dragon, has a problem. He wakes up one morning with a sniffy nose and a throat like sandpaper. Worst of all, he can't breathe any fire to cook his breakfast!

Cadwallader, his neighbour, certainly isn't going to share any of *his* breakfast. He sends Gribble off to see the dragon doctor. But what will Gribble do if the doctor cannot help?

This is the first title in a series of adventures about Gribble, the lovable little dragon.

0 552 52445X

YOUNG
CORGI

T.R. BEAR: ENTER T.R.

BY TERRANCE DICKS

It all started when Jimmy got a parcel from his Uncle Colin in America. The teddy bear inside was unlike any bear Jimmy had ever seen. He looked tough, and he was wearing glasses! According to the label, his name was Theodore Roosevelt – T.R. for short.

Life with T.R. is quite eventful as Jimmy and the other toys soon find out.

This is the first in a series of books about T.R.

0 552 523011

YOUNG
CORGI

T.R. BEAR: T.R AFLOAT

BY TERRANCE DICKS

'Sixteen men on a dead man's chest,' sang T.R.
Bear. 'Yo ho ho and a bottle of rum!'

Jimmy and T.R. are on holiday at last. On a
boat! The drive down and the first night on
board are quite an adventure in themselves. But
there's more excitement in store when T.R.
overhears two men plotting to steal some rare
birds' eggs from the island nature reserve.

He's determined to catch them red-handed. All
he needs is a plan . . .

0 552 524654

If you would like to receive a Newsletter about our new Children's books, just fill in the coupon below with your name and address (or copy it onto a separate piece of paper if you don't want to spoil your book) and send it to:

The Children's Books Editor
Young Corgi Books
61–63 Uxbridge Road,
Ealing
London W5 5SA

Please send me a Children's Newsletter:

Name . . . .

Address . . . .

. . . .

. . . .